DEEP
in the
HOLLER

Appalachian Tales

Elizabeth Hardin Buttke

Jan-Carol Publishing, Inc

"every story needs a book"

Deep in the Holler
Appalachian Tales
Elizabeth Hardin Buttke

Published January 2018
Little Creek Books
Imprint of Jan-Carol Publishing, Inc
All rights reserved
Copyright © 2018 by Elizabeth Hardin Buttke
Front Cover Painting: Helen Cook Lowe
Front Cover Design: Tara Sizemore

ISBN: 978-1-945619-53-3
Library of Congress Control Number: 2018935006

You may contact the publisher:
Jan-Carol Publishing, Inc
PO Box 701
Johnson City, TN 37605
publisher@jancarolpublishing.com
jancarolpublishing.com

To my family, thank you for all the memories.

Acknowledgments

Thank you to all the wonderful people who helped make this dream come true: my family for making my childhood a wonderful story; Lois Peterson, my dear aunt who gave me the inspiration to keep writing; Ron Hines, for the courage to publish my stories; Becky Lewis, who helped put some order to my writing and patiently reading each one. JCP, thank you for all your help, kindness and support.

The Blackberry Patch

I remember the days as if they were yesterday. The sun would come peeking over the mountain like a sleepy baby raising its head, trying to wake up. You could hear Mom clamoring and banging around in the kitchen getting breakfast ready, and the slam of the screen door as she went in and out. Me and my brothers lay like stretched-out cats on the beds in the room we shared, our little red heads peeking out from the top of the covers. "Hit the floor, young'uns," Mom would holler. "Hurry up, breakfast is ready. We're going to pick those blackberries before it gets hot."

Blackberries... Just to hear the word took all the fun out of sunshine and biscuits and gravy. Dragging out of bed, we moped to the table like lost puppies, hoping she would feel sorry for us and change her mind. It made me mad as a hornet that we had to do all the hard work so those little old ladies in town could make jelly and jam. "Hurry up and eat, then put some clothes on," Mom always was a go-getter; if there was nothing to do, she'd find something.

"How many we gotta pick?" we would ask, hoping it wasn't many.

"I got six gallons sold to Ms. Williams," she would say. Might as well have said two tons. Hearts would sink, mouths would droop. "Get ready, and I'll get the buckets." The boys would slowly pull on their pants and shoes, and I would slip my dress over my head. Then Mom would button or zip me up. The ole screen door would bang as each one of us came out and stood on the back porch. Mom handed each of us a lard bucket—she carried three with her—and off we'd march. Across the foot log, up the bank, and through the tobacco patch into the pasture.

Now if you've ever been to the blackberry patch, you know as good and well as I do it's no place to have any kind of fun. You get wet from the dew, right down to your shoes. Bees buzz from every direction, gnats fight over who's going to get in your eyes first, and lord help if you run up on a snake to boot. So here we'd go up the pasture, 'til Mom found a good place to start. Mom would place all of us in different spots with our buckets, and the dreaded picking would begin. If blackberries tasted good it wouldn't have been so bad—but wild blackberries are bitter, not tasty, to me. At first it wasn't so bad. Then, after a while of following an ole cow trail with weeds and briars all over, the dew starts making you just wet enough for your clothes to start sticking to you. By then the sun was out just high enough to hit you right in the eyes, but not to dry anything off. As hard as you tried to ease your hand in a bunch and out, somehow you got as many scratches as you did berries.

"Be sure you get all the ripe ones," Mom would holler. We didn't even feel like goofing off or talking, 'cause after a while you were damp, hot, and looked like you had been in a fight with a cat. After a rock of ages, the buckets were filled and here we'd come trudging back down the hill, looking like Br'er Rabbit that was thrown blindfolded into the briar patch. Just knowing you were done put a little skip in your step by the time you crossed the creek to the house.

I didn't much like the ride to town to sell the berries. Mom would put me in the back seat to make sure they didn't spill. Then up out of all of them buckets would come little ants, like there was a fire in the bottom. I'd be twisting and squirming trying my best to mash every one I'd see, hoping I hadn't missed any. Finally, it was done, the little lady had her berries and mom had her money. On the way home, with the wind blowing through the car and the sun on my face, I'd pray that God would just let the birds have the rest.

Apple Butter and Grandmother

Growing up, you were always hearing "back in the old days" stories. How hard it was, and how little they had. It just always seemed so interesting to me, and fun. Milking cows, churning butter, walking to school barefoot or in knee-deep snow. Everybody grew and canned their own food. Your meat came from your own animals, like chickens, pigs, and the cows you raised. I would listen to story after story, told by my mom's and my dad's parents, other kids' grandparents or parents. I never got tired of hearing 'bout the "good ole days."

It was because of this that one day I got a bright idea; I would talk my mom and grandmother—or Mamaw, as we called her—into making apple butter. Fall of the year was in full color, and wouldn't it be just cozy and fun to make apple butter? I didn't want the kind you made on the stove, now. No, I wanted the kind you make outside, in the big black pot over a fire. So finally, they both agreed to make a run, or batch, as they called it. They didn't act as excited as I did, but would do it to shut me up. First, Mamaw hunted down the big cast-iron pot; it reminded me of a witch's brewing pot. Then, we had to a have a stirring stick. This had a long wooden handle with a triangle-shaped piece on the end. We had to have lots of apples, all peeled and sliced. After a while, I was beginning to wonder what I had gotten myself into. But at last the apples were ready. I just couldn't wait to stir that big pot and pretend I was back in the old days. The morning air was a little chilly, and the smell of fall was crisp. The fire was built in my Mamaw's backyard, up near the clothesline. Even my aunt showed up to help. I let Mom and Mamaw get everything ready, and then we started cooking.

So, there we were. Mamaw was dressed in her polyester skirt, cotton blouse, and flannel shirt. Tall and slim, her black hair came right below her small ears, with just a hint of gray at the temples. Years of hard work and ten young'uns had just made her a strong, in-charge kind of woman. Then there was Mom, in a denim skirt, pullover shirt, and some old jacket she had thrown on. Her red hair was pinned up, and she'd tucked a chew of tobacco in her jaw. My aunt and I stood by, ready to begin. Everybody laughed and talked as we took turns stirring those apples and feeding the fire. Wow! I was making apple butter, just like in the old days! *How much better can it get?* I thought. Well, after standing and stirring, fetching wood, and adding apples half the day, I began to realize why they thought I was crazy for wanting to do this. It was slow and steady work, with the wind throwing ashes and smoke right in your face.

At last the apples were sauce, and it was time to take the big black pot to the back porch. There we would add the final flavoring, cinnamon. Took two of us to carry it, but there it sat, full and steaming hot, smelling like a fresh apple pie. Mamaw dives in the kitchen, rummaging around in the cabinets getting the cinnamon while Mom stirred. I'm watching, trying not to miss a thing. Here came Mamaw, like a bullet, With the lid in one hand and the small bottle in the other. She starts dashing it in, then all at once Mom and my aunt start yelling, "Mommy, stop! Stop!" As quick as it hit the pot, Mom's spoon was throwing it out. Hands were flying, all trying to grab the bottle.

"What's wrong?" Mamaw yelled, looking at everyone.

"That's *iodine*, not cinnamon," Mom said, as we all doubled over laughing. By then we were just sitting there trying to catch our breath.

"Well, good lord! I grabbed the wrong bottle," Mamaw laughed.

"Did you get it all?" my aunt asked, in between breaths.

Mom just laughed and shook her head, shrugging. "I think I did." So, we all looked to see if any of the orangey-red liquid was floating on top.

"Well, it won't hurt you," Mamaw said. Mom went back in the kitchen and got the cinnamon.

"Let's try this again," she laughed, and added the final ingredient to the apple butter.

It's been years; now, my mamaw is gone. But every time I see a jar of apple butter, I remember that day, and can see that big ole pot of apple butter, and iodine and apple sauce going in every direction. Now I have a back in the old days story of my own.

Just a Kid

Deep in the hills of the Flag Pond mountains, nestled at the bottom of a mountain, lived three little red headed kids. Two brothers and a sister. The house was small, just two bedrooms: one with a set of bunk beds and a full-sized bed, and one for Mom and Dad. A tall Warm Morning heater graced the living room, throwing out all the heat you needed on a cold winter night. An old cook stove stood in the kitchen in case the power went out. On a chilly fall morning, Mom would light the fire and cook breakfast. I guess Mom had fed everybody around there, and Dad always made sure you were warm—even if the candles melted off the wall, and I've seen them do it. But anybody that visited felt at home, and most times they didn't want to leave.

A creek ran out behind the house. In the summer it provided a cool swimming hole, and in the winter, it was a place to run and slide. Across the creek there was a field that joined the pasture and mountain. Our grandmother, an aunt, and an uncle lived spread out in a circle, within hollering distance. The main road ran in front of our house. My best friend lived right across the road, with her brother, mom, and stepdad.

Her grannie and papaw lived in a log house in the big yard almost touching hers. I remember her grannie, when a calf was born, would lock us and the calf in a stall away from its mom, and let us play with it for just a bit. Up the road just a piece was a little store, right off the road. Inside was all the necessary things, like bread, milk, sugar, flour, tobacco items, and a counter of glass and wood that was filled with chocolates, penny candy, and candy bars. Cold drinks filled the big square Coca-Cola cooler in the comer. If you had fifty cents you could get a drink, bag of chips, and five cents worth of penny candy. During the summer, when school was out and the days were long and lazy, we would all put our change together—a nickel, quarter, handful of pennies, whatever we had—and get drinks and candy to take up the mountain with us to play. There we'd go, five or six sets of bare feet traipsing up the pasture, dress tails and hair blowing in the wind, the boys carrying the goodies. We would pass the sweet apple tree, picking up a few, then walking on past the big rock into the mountains. We would pair off and build houses and forts, making our own pretend families and homes. Stumps made good chairs, moss was our carpet, and branches and ferns made a good roof, all held up on forked sticks. We survived blizzards, starvation, and floods— all make believe, of course, but real enough to us, just the same. Near supper time the voice of Mom or my aunt would sound in the distance, calling us in to eat.

Now, playhouses can be made out of lots of stuff. A wood shed, old toilet, hog pen, anything with walls and a door. Add a baby doll, or a large gourd if you didn't have one, some discarded dishes and a few flowers, and you've set up housekeeping. And when you got tired of that you had a church, store, school house, just whatever you wanted it to be. I've seen some pretty good church services with brother Hardin calling the lost souls to repent while sister Lamb banged a sorrowful tune on the little wooden piano. Baby dolls cried and little mothers tried to hush them. But every once in a while, somebody had to play the deceased: usually brother Dale or Steve, since they fell by the wayside so much. Then the saddest funeral ever would be held. Preacher Hardin decided whether you went to heaven or burned forever. Just had to hope he was in a loving spirit that day.

For some reason, no matter how much fun you were having, it was always better to meet at the branch or behind the wood pile and puff on a cigarette. These were usually taken when and where ever a grown up laid a pack down. We'd fight over who got to light it, then pass it around like a hot potato. Heads would turn like a scared chicken to make sure nobody was coming. I always thought it was funny that no matter how sick or dizzy you got, you'd be right there the next time the ole cig was fired up. Soon the sun would start going down. Everybody darted in different directions going home. Lying in bed at night all tired and sleepy, you would never imagine that one day you'd give anything to just be a kid.

Birthday Money

You know, there's just some things in life you don't forget. Things that later are some of your fondest memories. One of my favorites is the birthday cards my Aunt Lois use to send me. A month before my birthday, I would start watching the mail. I mean, getting a card (or any mail) at a young age makes you feel like you're really important. And when there's money inside, well...it just don't get any better. So, at the first of August that year, I started watching the mail.

Every day after school, I would rush in and ask Mom, "Did I get a card yet?"

She'd say, "Not yet," and I would sigh and wait some more. After what seemed like a trillion days, she would finally say "Yes," and I would fly to open it, read every word, and count my money. Then I'd walk around hearing my brothers whine about how they never got a card, which made me feel even more special. The ole goats didn't deserve one, mean things that they were. But I never knew that one night I'd be pouring out my soul and crying like a baby to save my birthday money.

It all started one evening right after dark. Me and my younger brother, and a friend up the road, wanted to play cops and robbers. Since it was one girl against two boys, I got the BB gun. The boys started running and hiding, yelling "You'll never get us!" So I loaded the gun, gave it a few good pumps, and took off after them. I saw them dive into Dad's old garage. Sneaking around my older brother's car, I ran in on them.

"Got you!" I yelled.

Then someone whispers real loud, "Shoot the gun! Here comes a car!" I leaned out the garage door and just pulled the trigger, not aiming at all. *Bing!* That's all we heard. Standing still as church mice, we looked around. *Oh god, what did I hit?* was all I thought, 'cause that BB gun had already gotten me in enough trouble.

"Come with me boys, and help me look; it's *dark,*" I pleaded. We crept down the driveway, and in the glorious moonlight I saw it. The back window in my brother's pride and joy of a car was shattered. Fear ran from my toenails to the top of my head. And of course, when something like this happens, the helpers run like a brush fire was in their pants to tell on you, to save their own skin. My first thought was run to safety. And where was that? Right in the middle of the bed, between Mom and Dad. I dove into that bed like an arrow.

"What in the world?!" was all my mom got out before the bedroom light was on and my brother was trying to tear me out of the bed.

Mom and Dad were hollering, I was crying, and all I could hear was, "I want *all* her birthday money; she shot my back window out of my car!" *Oh, no... not my birthday money!* I had waited a year for that, and no way was I giving that up for a car window! So, I cried and pleaded, "No, not my birthday money, please!" Mom finally got him to hush, and I explained what had happened. My dad got up and found the BB gun. I lay behind Mom, crying. Dad took the gun out in the back yard and beat it against the tree 'til it fell to pieces, and threw the pieces in the creek. Things calmed down, I got to keep my money, and my brothers hated me for a while. We were never allowed to have another BB gun after that.

Sundays

My mom and dad were what I called Strict Free Will Baptist. No TV, radio, deck of cards, or anything that might lead to trouble was allowed in the house. I was taught to keep my dress down below my knees and act like a lady. We went to church faithfully, and sometimes held prayer meetings in people's homes. Most Sundays we either went to a preacher's house for dinner, or their family would come to ours. Sometimes after dinner we would go visit old folks or someone who was sick, or so Mom and Dad could talk and wait 'til church time. My dad was always helping somebody, and Mom was always feeding somebody. But being a little kid, you don't see the importance of all this until you're older. We'd get bored, or sometimes carsick riding across curvy mountain roads, stopping to let one of us puke. All day, we were hoping the preacher would want to cut it short and get home too, or wasn't, as some would say, a long-winded preacher.

I remember one particular Sunday morning, me, my two brothers, and our mom and dad loaded up in the car and headed to church. Now, the minute you get out of the car at church, Mom would automatically give us "the look," and say, "You better be good, or I'll get you when we get home." And trust me, you knew she would.

Now, I can't remember exactly what we had done this time, but all three of us had done something. Maybe we had popped our chewing gum, or got tickled or fidgety. Who knows, but when we got in the car we were all promised a whipping when we got to the house. Oh, the dread: wanting to be first but hoping you'd be last, when the time came. We hardly breathed all the way home.

At the time, we lived in a little trailer while Dad was building the house in front of it. When we got there, we dragged out of the car and Mom went to get the switch. She handed it to Dad and told him to take us in the house one at a time. Dad was going to whip us! This was bad; he'd never whipped me. The boys came out one then the other, crying and half mad. "Come on, Sissy," Dad said. My head was down, hands wringing in the front, no bigger than a grasshopper and my little maxi dress shaking like a leaf. I followed him into the half-built kitchen and stood there crying and shaking, waiting. He was trying to explain why I was getting the whipping, and I agreed to everything he said, never looking up. Then he took my little hand gently and he walked me back to the trailer.

"Did you whup her?" Mom asked.

"I can't whup her; she was standing there shaking and crying, and looked just like a little old lady." He grinned. "I can't do it." Could it be they was going to feel sorry for their only little girl, and not whip me? Nope.

"Well if you can't then I will," Mom said. "If the boys get one, then so does she." Mom made sure I got mine, too. After that, when I'd get in trouble, I'd beg Mom to let Dad whip me. I never won that plea, 'cause she knew what I had in mind, and that he wouldn't. But I can say I don't regret a-one I got. They weren't beatings, just a few stings around the legs—enough to make you think twice about not minding or doing something wrong. And my daddy never did try to whip me again. He left that to Mom.

A Bear Dog and
a Coffee Can

My mamaw had ten children. The youngest one, of course, was petted to death. By the time he had graduated high school, all his brothers and sisters had married and had kids of their own. All of them doted on my uncle, and he was always Mamaw's baby. My uncle worked a lot out of town when he was older. He mostly let Mamaw take care of things around home, since he didn't have a wife, and he just lived at the other end of the tobacco field.

He loved his freedom, and hunting was his passion. I remember on one occasion, he had just bought a new hound pup—paid a lot of money for him, too. His hopes were to make a fine bear dog out of him. Every hunter wanted the best hound, and to have bragging rights. Right after my uncle got this pup, he was called to go out of town to work. So of course, he got dear ole Mamaw to look after him while he was gone. "Just make sure you water and feed him," he said as he left, and Mamaw waved as he went down the driveway.

Every day she walked out the field to his house and watered and fed the pup. Then one day, she stepped out in the backyard, and there the pup stood. *Well, how did you get loose?* she thought. *You're probably thirsty.* She fumbled around in the can house and came back out with an old tin coffee can. Going to the spigot, she ran some water in the can for it. Sure enough, the pup dove its head right in, lapping up the water. She picked up her basket of wet sheets and headed to the clothesline above the grapevines. She could hear coffee can and hound banging around below her in the yard while she strung sheets across the line. Coming back down to the yard, she noticed the can was still on the dog's head, and he didn't look like he was having fun, either. *Well, for goodness sakes,* she thought. *What's it doing?* Setting the empty basket down, she grabbed him from behind and tried to pull his head free of the can, but it wouldn't budge. The more she pulled, the more it yelped and cried. The can was stuck, and stuck good. When she let go to try something else the pup took off, feet tearing at the ground and the can beating like a drum.

By then my mom was there, and both of them were trying to run it down. Up the yard, down the yard, through the field and back. Finally, the pup collapsed and didn't move. Now they're both trying to pull its head free. Working together, they finally got the coffee can off, but the poor thing had suffocated. "It's dead," my mom said.

"Oh, my lord," Mamaw said. "He's going to kill me; he wouldn't take nothing for this thing." Both of them sat there in the yard out of breath, looking at the would have been bear dog. "Come on," Mamaw told Mom. "We'll have to bury it somewhere; he won't find out." Up behind the wood shed they dug the grave and put him in. "Nobody better not ever tell him, either," Mamaw said.

My uncle always thought he had gotten loose and ran off or somebody had stolen him, and Mamaw never told him different.

Bird Hill

As you came up the road through the mountain—right when you got out of what we called the S-curves—if you looked to your left, past the apple orchard, there sat a white house above the pasture, tucked nicely into the hills. I don't know exactly how we came up with the name. One of us kids must have spit it out one day, and it stuck. Bird Hill, that's what we called it. A long winding dirt road followed the bank across a wooden bridge, and around to the top of the hill to the house.

One of my best friends lived there, with her mom, two sisters, and two brothers. I used to hate spending the night in the winter. It would be so cold in the mornings, with snow on the ground, and we would have to walk that long little road all the way to the main road. Then we had to stand there and wait on the bus. And in a dress, that was *cold*! But we all had so much fun, and they were no different than my own family. In the summer, when school was out, we would sit on the cool concrete steps of the front porch, looking down on the road, watching the few cars come and go as we painted our finger-nails for the hundredth time. Or we would spend most of the day reading Harlequin romance books, and talking about our own puppy love. If we got bored we would walk up to my house, which was about a mile on up the main road, and see what was going on there. Most of the time we'd all team up with everybody and play basketball there in the driveway, where dad had put us up a goal.

Even though we were only maybe twelve or thirteen, my mom or hers would let us drive their car to her house, or mine sometimes. But one day, when we were couple years older, we crashed her mom's car into a culvert. We were coming down the road and it had rained. I was puffing on a cigarette, and we were going to turn around. Well, she cut off the road a little too fast. When the tires hit the wet grass, it just shot us into that deep ditch, nose first. We got out of the car, shaking; she was about to cry, 'cause she knew her mom would be furious. Then she looks at me and says, "How are you still smoking that cigarette?!"

"I don't know," I answered blankly, staring at the rear end of the car sticking up in the air.

"Well, give me a puff," she demanded. "I gotta calm down!" Of course, the man way across the road had heard us hit, and came over to make sure we were all right. And to offer to pull the crippled old car home. We didn't drive her mom's car after that, when she got another one. We didn't even realize how hard it had been for her to get the car, or how hard it would be to get another one.

It didn't help that one day my dear friend decided she was tired of only having a few clothes to wear, and wanted more—even though her and her mom went around and around about not having money for more. Plus, the other four didn't get new clothes, so why should she? She thought for a couple days and came up with a solution to solve that problem. "Come on," she said, after everybody left that Saturday to go to town.

"What are you going to do?" I asked. In the bedroom she went, gathering up all her clothes. I followed her out to the back yard, to the barrel they burned their trash in. Into the barrel went all her clothes, a dash of kerosene, and a match.

As the flames ate up the armload of clothes, she grinned and said, "'Now she'll *have* to buy me some!" Of course we watched them burn, her just a-grinning and me thinking, *What the heck has she done?* It wasn't so funny when her mom got home. First thing she did was send me home. Then her mom gave her a good dose of hickory tea; we all know what *that* is. She wore the clothes on her back 'til school started, too. Bird Hill...now, that was an exciting place.

When you look up there now, coming up the road, there's a different house, different family. The old dirt road is paved, the wooden bridge is gone. But I still see the white house, the dirt road, and us sitting on the front porch.

Nothing to worry about, except what color of polish we were going to paint our nails with next.

The Cry Baby

My grandmother had just gotten all the children and herself tucked into bed that night when the storm rolled in. The two-story house, sitting above the creek, was lit up as lighting flashed across the dark sky. Thunder rolled, making a rumbling sound as it came through the holler. Then the rain came, beating the old tin roof like a team of horses. Everyone lay quietly in their beds listening to the wind and pouring rain. After a while my mamaw and papaw got up and went outside on the porch to see if there was anything to worry about. Of course, when the young'uns heard the screen door shut, they got up to see what was going on.

There all of them stood on the porch, gown tails a-blowing in the wind, everybody looking at the sky. *Sure enough, it was going to be a good one*, everybody thought. The trees were swaying and the yard was running in little rivers. One good thing about it, they wouldn't be no hoeing tomorrow; that brought a few smiles. Papaw lit a cigarette and blew the thin blue smoke out into the night. Somewhere, almost hidden in the sounds of the storm, came a different sound. "What was that?" one of the girls asked.

"Shhh," my grandmother whispered, and they all turned their good ear to listen.

"You hear that?" one of the boys said.

"Sounds like a baby crying."

"Really?!" the girls asked, all big-eyed. Now all the girls were looking a little spooked and scared. Once again, just below the sound of the wind, came the faint cry of a baby, a little louder than the first. Now the girls were crying, begging Papaw or the boys to get down to the creek to see if they could see it, or hear it better and save it.

"Hush," Mamaw said.

"Why?!" they wailed. "It's going to die if you don't go!"

"No, it ain't; that baby died a long time ago," Mamaw said.

"*What?!*" they shrieked, looking plumb wild-eyed. So Mamaw began telling the story.

"Long time ago, there was a flood and a baby got swept away. Now and then, on certain stormy nights, you can hear its cries." Goose bumps crawled up all the young'uns now and they begged to hear the whole story.

"Let's get in the house," Papaw said, and nobody argued with that. After closing the door, they all gathered around to hear the rest of the story.

"One time, years ago," Mamaw started, "a young married couple lived a little ways up the creek, on the other side. Soon the girl and young man had a little baby. But one night, it started raining, and raining hard. In no time the creek started rising, fast. The poor girl, being young, tried to make it to the barn to get in the loft with the baby. The water pulled and tugged at her as she fought her way towards the barn, holding the baby tight. But somehow, she lost her footing. Quick as a flash, the water took the baby out of her arms. That poor baby was never found."

The girls were wiping their eyes and looking at each other all sorrowful. "That's why you can still hear it cry sometimes," Mamaw said. "Now, let's all get to bed."

It took a while for them to settle down again, but sleep finally overtook them. Every time it rained after that, they would listen; only a few ever heard it again growing up.

My First Chew

Growing up, I think my mom and dad's theory was that a self-taught lesson was a lesson truly learned. Which sometimes can be a good thing— in my case, one time it was a horrible thing. Mom and dad didn't smoke, and alcohol was considered the "devil's brew." But my mom chewed, and she chewed the strong stuff, too: good ole Samson. She always had half a twist of it in her skirt pocket. As she went about her day, her mouth worked as hard as she did. If a bee stung you or something bit you, tobacco juice would cure it. She'd take her finger, spit on it, and rub it on.

Now, most girls back then wanted to follow in their mom's footsteps, so of course, I did, too. I wanted to get married, have me some kids, take care of my house, cook and clean. One nice, hot summer day, when I was seven, mom decided I could start learning to wash dishes. The trailer we lived in while Dad was building the house was hot as an oven. She put a kitchen chair up to the sink and helped me get started, tying a towel around my waist to keep my dress from getting wet. If you got the belly of your dress wet you would marry a drunk, was what I was always told.

Being up in that chair, I felt as old and wise as her. I squared my shoulders, puffed out like a momma hen with doodles, and started washing dishes. Then it hit me; *I need a chew of that tobacco! Then I'll for sure be a woman.* So, I turned around and asked mom for a chew. Now, in my mind I thought this meant I was growing up, and she thought so too. Who wouldn't? Reaching into her skirt pocket, she pulled the tobacco twist out with a little grin. "You sure you want this?" she asked. "Yeah," I answered. She broke off a little piece and put it between my gum and cheek, telling me not to swallow any juice. I was washing and chewing, waiting to spit my first stream of juice. In Mom's mind, it was a way to break me from ever picking up a bad habit. But that was her little secret.

With the little chew tucked safely in my jaw, I kept washing. After a while, I noticed it had got hotter. Sweat was breaking out all over me. The bitter tobacco started to get stronger in my mouth, and the sink was swaying. Mom must have been watching, 'cause she asked me what was wrong. "I don't feel so good," I said, shaking and pale. "And I feel like I'm going to puke."

I melted down in the chair and looked up at her. *Why is this funny to her?* I thought, getting sicker by the second. She grinned and held out her hand. "Spit that tobacco out, Sissy," she said, and held her hand out while I spit and gagged it out into her hand. Then it dawned on me that the tobacco was what had made me sick! I was crying, drunk as a buzzard, and weak as the dish water. We went to the bathroom, and I spit and spit while she held a cold washrag to my forehead and neck. Oh, I was so sick! I just *knew* I was dying.

"You'll be all right," she said. "Just lay down for a bit, and hold this rag on your head." I laid there a long time, 'til it passed and then some.

After that, she didn't have to say, "I hope this taught you a lesson," or "I better not catch you chewing after this." Forty-some years later, there has never been another chew in my mouth. I learned my lesson well. And I forgot about growing up, real fast.

Fried Chicken

It was a beautiful Sunday morning when my mamaw woke up. The birds were singing, and sunshine glittered off the morning dew in the yard as she gazed out her bedroom window. Everyone rushed to get the morning chores done: cow milked, eggs gathered, and stove wood brought in for the cook stove. After a hardy breakfast, she scrubbed faces and combed hair with the help of the older children, then headed for church. The walk to church was peaceful. Everyone stopped and took the time to pluck a honeysuckle bloom and savor the sweet taste. Some walked, some raced. But Mamaw brought them all back in line like a mother hen.

Coming home, they chattered away. Mamaw turned to one of the older boys to give him orders for when they got home, to find a fat hen and kill it for Sunday dinner. "One of the girls will help you scald and pluck it," she said. When they got in the front door, everyone scattered to change clothes and do the chores for dinner. Throwing on an apron, she was about to get started when Papaw spoke up to tell her family was walking across the mountain to eat dinner and spend a little time with them. Adding up in her head, she averaged out how much more food she'd have to make. Years of experience had made her an expert at putting a meal together with very little time.

Soon the chicken was frying, the biscuits a-baking, and the girls were setting the table. The uncle and aunt, plus all the little cousins, were smiling and laughing, having a good time. "Time to eat," she called as she spooned the last of the chicken gravy into the bowl. Everyone gathered at the table to say grace. The table steamed with all the good food, and the plate of fried chicken sat brown and crispy in the middle of it all. My uncle, a young boy at the time, sat quietly, waiting for the food to be passed. Finally, his aunt handed him the plate of chicken and asked him if he wanted a leg. He looked up at her, bewildered.

After a moment of awkward silence, he replied, "I didn't know there *was* anything but a neck."

"Lord, Honey," his aunt laughed, "take a leg today."

Mamaw's face turned every color of red while all the adults laughed. He grabbed the neck and passed the plate on quick, a little embarrassed himself. He was too small to know that all the good parts of the chicken were usually taken by the adults before the plate reached the children.

I don't think any of us sit down to eat chicken, to this day, that we don't smile and remember seeing my uncle, looking confused and embarrassed.

The Wood Stove

Growing up, everybody I knew had a wood stove. Some, like us, had one in the front room and a cook stove in the kitchen. The sound of a chain saw, or the chop of an ax, was a song of its own, just like the birds singing. At the first hint of fall, men started getting their winter wood ready. They worked with the speed of a squirrel gathering nuts, hauling, chopping, and stacking the stove wood. But I don't think anybody got as excited as my dad did about building the first fire of the season. And boy, could he make that ole stove walk the dog, as we used to say. He wouldn't have any stove but a Warm Morning, and trust me they were a good stove; he still has one.

You could go to this one's or that one's house, and it would either be comfy warm, or warm around the stove, but a little drafty in the back rooms. Not our house. It wasn't warm, it was *hot!* Not just the front room, either, but every room, crack, and corner. My best friend wouldn't even spend the night in the winter, 'cause she got so hot she'd get sick and throw up. My brother's friend was found asleep one morning in the floor at the front door, I guess trying to get some cool air from the crack at the bottom of the door. Us kids were sorta used to it. We just laid there and sweated it out. Nope, you wouldn't get cold at our house, I don't care how low the temperature dropped.

My mom had a mirror on the wall, and on each side of it was a candle holder. She'd put candles in, and the next morning they would be hanging down like the icicles on the edges of the tin roof outside. We could hear the creak of the stove door when it opened, listening to hear how many sticks went in. Mom would holler, "Don't pile it full, let that burn down some."

"I'm just going to lay one stick," Dad would say. But of course, he couldn't stop at one. Sometimes us young'uns would take turns walking by and dashing a cup of water in the stove, hoping it would put it out.

Nowadays he has an oil stove, and most days it's just right in the house. But when the forecast says temperatures will fall in the teens at night, he banks the old Warm Morning that now sits in the closed-in back porch. Then he waits for Mom to give the OK to light the fire. I can firmly say, I was never cold growing up. I didn't have to worry about how cold it was outside, or how much it snowed.

'Cause trust me, we were as toasty as bread in the oven.

The Station Wagon

My dad always was the type that believed you made do with what you had. Didn't matter if you could afford better, use what you got first. For instance, my mom wanted a picture window; so dad took a sliding glass door that was laying around, popped it in sideways, and presto—there was her picture window. Need a door knob? He'd nail an empty spool—yes, from a spool of thread—to the door, and there was your door knob.

He was also a trader of watches, knives and sometimes cars. I assume this is how we ended up with the green station wagon. It was a nice-enough looking car. Lots of room to sit, plus space in the back for hauling stuff, too.

My oldest brother was a young teenager at the time. So he and his friends would camp out in the back of the wagon in the yard, while me and my younger brother, along with some friends, would pester them all night. Of course, he would pitch a fit; that kind of stuff just cramped his style, at his age.

One day, he came home from school all excited to tell mom he had been approved to work that summer, with a program at school that let kids work and earn money during summer break. Of course, Dad would drop him off and pick him up at the school, since the job he had at the time was flexible and mom didn't work or have a car.

Overnight, my brother became a man: a *working* man. Time to start shaving, throwing on some cologne, fixing his hair, and acting all bossy and stuff. Eventually he had eyes on the girls who worked with him. Made friends from town, not like us country folk. But we just looked over him, and Dad continued to drive him back and forth.

One day my day was off from work, piddling around, and had this great idea to turn his station wagon into a car-slash-truck. Mom ranted and raved, but she couldn't talk him out of it, so the project began. Heck, me and my younger brother thought it was an awesome idea; we couldn't wait to ride in the back, just like a truck. Dad worked 'bout all day in that old garage he had. And then there it was: a piece of plywood, and plexiglass made the back window...he had out done himself this time 'cause he had put metal porch railings down each side of the bed.

Now, who'd have thought you could take porch railings and do that! Mom had a fit, and swore she'd never ride in it. But me and little brother couldn't wait for our first ride. Soon, it was time to pick up the working man. We begged Dad to let us go, and to make it better, he put two metal folding chairs in the back for us to sit on. Here we went, grinning from ear to ear, warm wind blowing in our face, red hair flying everywhere.

We made it to town and pulled up to the school, stopping where the other parents were parked, waiting on their kids. My dad was just as proud as if he was driving a new truck, and we couldn't wait for our brother to get his first ride.

Slowly, the big yellow school bus came to a screeching halt. The door swung open and all the teenagers clambered off, saying bye and leaving—and there stood my brother. You could have lit a cigarette off his face. He ducked so low he might as well had crawled to the car, and dove into the front seat. "Get out of here, Dad, and fast," he said, "before everybody sees us." Dad just laughed and started home. We couldn't hear what else was said in the car. We just stretched out and enjoyed the ride home. We thought he just didn't want to messed up his hair.

After we got home, my brother made it clear he'd walk from then on before he'd ride in that contraption and have everybody thinking we was crazy. But the poor guy knew he didn't have a choice. So later that evening, he begged Dad to park far enough away when he dropped him off and picked him up that nobody would see, and he'd walk the short distance to the bus. My dad just laughed, but told him he would; and he did, to my brother's relief. Soon the summer ended, and it wasn't long 'til he had his own car. But to us, it would never be as cool as Dad's car/truck

CANDY CORN

Prologue

Sheriff Harris knelt down beside the small body that lay crum-
pled on the ground. He felt the dampness of the evening
dew seep through the knee of his pants. Fred, his only deputy,
stood back a-ways, feeling sick at what he saw.

"Who is it, Boss?" he asked.

The sheriff took a deep breath. "I won't know for sure 'til
I turn him over and see the face," he answered. He raised his
head and looked around as if hoping someone would step out
of the trees and say, "I did that; it was me." But the only sounds
he heard were the creek and the light breeze coming through
the woods. How huge his hand looked as he placed it on the
back, covered in only what used to be a white cotton t-shirt.

Come on Bill, he thought. *Do it quick, and get it over.* The
little body had gotten stiff, and was bluish pale. "Oh, my god,
Fred cried, as the face of the child came into view. "It's little

Jodie, Earl and Rosie's little boy." Then he turned his head and vomited the shock and disgust up from his belly.

The sheriff's shoulders shook, a tear rolling down his cheek as he looked at the boy's face. His soft blonde hair had a mixture of dried mud and leaves in it. The eyes were closed, as if he was asleep. Except for the t-shirt, he had only hand-sewn undergarments on. No overalls, pants, or whatever he had worn, were around.

"What's that stuff on the corners of his mouth, Sheriff?" He turned to see Fred squatting and pointing to what looked like dried orange spit at the corners of the slightly parted lips. Bending down, he took his finger and tried to open the mouth some, with no luck. "Bless his heart," Fred said. "Looks like the little feller was eating candy when it happened."

The sheriff said, "I'm sick all over, Fred. Come on; let's get him to Doc Vance's house, and see what he can tell us."

Gently, they wrapped little Jodie in Sheriff Harris' worn denim coat. "I'll carry him. You lead the way, Fred. It's going be dark in a bit, so let's get out of here: don't like the feeling of the dark."

It seemed like it took forever to get back to the dirt road. The battered ole car the county had finally got for them sat like a hearse now, waiting. Opening the back door, they laid the small bundle on the back seat, tucking the coat in. Somehow, it made them feel better. And soon the car and passengers were going out the road in a cloud of dust that blew up behind them. Neither one spoke or looked back.

Chapter 1

The weathered porch swing moved slow an easy. I sat there and watched the evening sun cast a peaceful glow as it was going down. The light breeze lifted the dust some on the worn path through the yard to the road. Getting up, I walked to the plank steps and sat down, resting my chin in my hands.

Looking down the road, I saw old Jim making his way up the road towards home. His dusty gray hat sat a little crooked on his balding head, and as usual, his thin worn overalls looked in need of a wash.

"Whatcha doing, Lily?" he asked, and grinned toothlessly.

"Just waiting on Momma and Daddy to get back," I answered.

"Found another one, did they?" he asked. By now the word was all over the mountain. He put his hand into his pocket and pulled out a piece of gum.

"I reckon so," I said, walking through the yard to the road so he could hear me better.

"Here..." He reached me the gum. I unwrapped it, stuck it in my mouth, and began to chew.

"Well, you get back on the porch and wait there, I'm going to head on home. Maybe I'll hear something on up the road."

"OK. I'll see you later, Jim." Throwing up his hand, he went on up the road. Back in the yard, I hopped back on the porch and began swinging and chewing the sweet gum, waiting. *Old Jim, I thought. Just as poor as the rest of us, but always giving the young'uns a little something when you saw him. Too bad he don't have any family to look after him. Maybe tomorrow Momma can make an extra loaf of bread, and I'll drop it off to him.*

Dark was setting in now, so I went in, put some more wood into the cook stove, and turned on the lamp by the door. I guess I should have been a little scared all by myself, with all the horrible things going on. But being an only child, I had learned to not pay attention to a lot of things when I was by myself. The clock on the mantel had struck eight when I heard the Ford truck groaning up beside the house. Jumping up, I ran to the back door. Dad got out and come around the truck to help momma open the squeaky truck door. I could see she'd been crying, and her little bun on the back of her head had come loose some.

Taking her elbow, he led her into the house while I held the screen door open. Quietly I let it shut. "Just sit there at the table Mary; I'll heat up some coffee," Dad said. Sitting down, she waved me over to her lap and I sat down, laying my head on her shoulder while she hugged me tight, stroking my long brown hair gently. Dad sat opposite of us and reached out to pat her arm. "Don't worry, Mary. We'll get them, whoever it is. Everybody's just going to have to work together and keep a close eye on the young'uns around here."

"I know," she whispered, "but it's so scary and sad—especially for the families, Bud."

"I know, I know," Dad's voice soothed. Getting up, he poured two steaming-hot cups of black coffee. We sat there in silence. I didn't even ask Momma what happened.

After washing the cups, Momma led me through the house while Dad cut the light off and locked the doors. She tucked me in, kissing me on the forehead and looked deep into my face.

"Lily, me and your dad don't want you going off alone anymore. It's not safe right now. So you mind your momma, you hear?"

"Yes, Momma," I whispered. "Who was it?" And again, she started crying.

"Oh, Honey," she said, wiping the tears away. "It was little Jodie." All of a sudden, the air was sucked from my chest. I knew I wanted to cry, but it was like a door had slammed closed on my chest. *Little Jodie,* my mind raced.

What would Aunt Rosie do? He was only four: just a baby! There really was a monster out there. I jumped into my momma's arms, and the tears fell like rain.

"It's OK," she whispered.

"Is he dead, Momma?" I asked.

"Yes, Honey; just like Teddy, Ada and John's little boy."

"Does somebody just not like little boys?" I asked

"I don't know, but that's two in four months. Please promise me you won't wander off alone or visit anybody alone, OK?"

"OK," I promised, with gasps between my sobs.

"Now get some sleep. We have to get up early and go help aunt Rosie. Uncle Earl will need us, too."

When the light was turned out, I started feeling scared for the first time in a long time. Maybe the monster was watching me! I slid a little deeper under the covers, and lay there while my thoughts raced.

Chapter 2

Earlier that evening, Doc Vance had just sat down to eat supper when the sheriff came pounding on the door. Getting up, he walked through the house to the small room he used as an office. Opening the door, he saw the sheriff standing there with the small bundle in his arms. Fred was close behind him. The doctor didn't have to ask. He spread a clean white sheet on the wooden examining table.

"Just lay him down there, boys," he motioned to the sheriff and Fred. Two little dirty feet peeked out from the old coat. The doctor slowly opened the front of the coat. The two men now stood in the far corner, looking hard at the floor. *Don't blame them*, the doctor thought. *As old as I am, I'm not used to seeing stuff like this myself.* "Where did you find him, Bill?" he asked the sheriff.

"Down by the creek, 'bout a mile past JD's corn field. What do you think happened, Doc?"

"Well, Bill, from what I can see, he's had something around his neck: been strangled. There's bruising all around. Also, you can see were somebody has held him down, because they left bruising from their fingers on his upper arms." Doc Vance then gently laid the boy over on his stomach. He finished removing the torn, soiled undergarment with a pair of scissors.

The small-boned shoulders were bruised all the way across. Looking lower, he saw the intent of this attack, just like the other boy. The boys bottom looked like someone had beat him. It hurt the doctor to even look. Some of the flesh was black from the force that had been used. Rape, plain and simple.

Lord, I wonder what the little fella thought as he was going through all this. In all his years of practice, the doctor had never seen what torment really looked like—until he had to examine this little boy, and the other one. Turning him back over, the doctor wanted to check one more thing. Sure enough, the same pale orange spit was settled around the mouth. Looking over his glasses at the sheriff, he stated hard and plain, "You got a heartless, sick man out there, Sheriff. You better find him before some of the families do, or you're going to have a mess on your hands."

"We've been trying, Doc, but we can't put a finger on who around these parts would ever do such a thing. Maybe a drifter has slipped in somewhere."

"People around here are just poor farming families. All they have is each other, so why would any of them hurt their own? I don't know Sheriff, but you better find them," the doc warned.

Earl and Rosie didn't even bother to knock They busted through the door, but came to a sudden halt when they saw the look on the faces of the men. "Where is he?" they asked weakly.

"Come here, Earl. You too, Rosie," the sheriff spoke to them gently. They moved with all the strength they had to the table that held their baby. Fred caught Rosie before she hit the floor. Doc Vance quickly got the smelling salts. Sheriff Harris placed his hands on Earl's shoulders as his body shook with sobs.

"Oh my god!" he cried. "Look what he did to my little boy! Please, lord, don't let it be true." But sadly, it was. The only sounds in the room were the moans and cries of their broken hearts as they looked, touched, and kissed their son on his little cheeks. It seemed like eternity before they were able to leave.

"I'll bring him on up to your house, Earl," the sheriff offered.

"No," Rosie stated firmly. "I'll take him."

"Let me help you, Rosie." Sheriff Harris lifted the body and carried it out to the car they had borrowed, placing him in his mamma's arms.

"I'm so sorry. I'll catch them, I promise," he said. Rosie's face had turned to stone, and he knew she didn't even hear him.

Fred helped Earl into the back seat. "I'm going to drive them; he ain't able. I'll just walk home afterward," Fred explained.

"OK," the sheriff agreed. "I'll pick you up there later. We'll go on over to the office for a bit."

The sheriff and Fred hung around the office 'til the night chill forced them inside. Leaning back in his chair, the sheriff stared off into space.

"What do you think we should do next, Bill?" Fred asked.

"I think we will go back to the creek, scout around the area, see if we can find anything we might have overlooked," Sheriff Harris answered. "Look for tracks left by the person, or the rest of that young'un's clothes. Heck, Fred, he didn't even have his socks or shoes on! Just like that little Teddy boy, no britches or overalls, either. They have to be somewhere. Then I'm going to get Clem and some of his boys to look for any camps or places someone might have spent the night, then high tailed it out of here. I'll tell old Jim while he's sitting down at the store, or moseying around, to keep his eyes and ears open, too."

"You know, Bill, both them boys had the same kind of candy in their mouth. Makes me wonder if somebody ain't bribing them with it, to lure them off by theirselves," Fred stated.

"That makes sense, Fred. Neither one of the mothers had given them money for the store. I'll see if Willard remembers anybody buying any recently, down at the store. We will tell the families to make sure the kids walk together to school, and stay close together."

"Well, something better turn up, or we're going to be known as the mountain that went to pieces in the nineteen thirties!" Fred declared, then got up to take his anger out on the stove wood.

Later, lying in his bed, the sheriff's mind raced, filled with visions of things he would never forget. His heart broke for the suffering those babies had to endure. Over in the deep holler, a father lay on the cold night ground, broken and help-less. His tears mixed with the earth beneath him. Soon the frost covered him, along with the trees, grass, and housetops. But he was already numb. Sorrow has no respect of person. It loves the poor as much as the rich. It's a friend to the young as well as the old. The same with evil.

On this same night, lying in another bed of madness and foul smells, the monster was still trying to calm the excitement that surged through his veins. Sweat ran off his body as his nose sniffed the air, trying to capture one last scent of his feast. He reached for the jar, drinking with a great thirst. Soon a different heat came over him. Closing his eyes, his thoughts fell through a tunnel of darkness. The room was as cold as the form that lay on the bed.

Chapter 3

The funeral was awful. Aunt Rosie had to be held up by uncle Earl and Dad. Uncle Earl could barely stand himself. There's just something unnatural 'bout seeing a little boy or girl lying in a wooden box. Sorta looks like a doll laying there. It's a mixture of sweet and haunting. You never forget it. The face sticks in your mind like a bad nightmare. You want to forget it, but you want to remember it, too.

At the tender age of eight, my mind absorbed every detail.

The grannie women had fixed Jodie. His lips and cheeks were now raspberry red. His blonde hair had been washed and combed to the side. A new blue plaid shirt was buttoned all the way up to hide the marks. The men stood with hardened faces and the women sobbed and groaned while the preacher said a few words over the coffin. Most of the young'uns couldn't bear to look; they hid their faces in their mommas' dress tails or their daddys' pants legs. All I could think was *poor little Jodie*. No more climbing trees together, playing hide and seek in the barn, or swimming in the creek. His brothers and sister wouldn't get to see their baby brother ever again. A couple of neighborhood men walked slowly to the wooden coffin, placing the lid on. Aunt Rosie slid to the ground, moans like a wounded animal lifted high above the sound of the hammer as the nails were driven in, sealing her baby in darkness. Afterward, Dad took my hand and we started walking down the worn path from the grave yard. Momma and Aunt Rosie were still looking down that dark hole.

Back at the house, us kids sat quietly under the big maple tree, each one deep in our own thoughts. Tom, James, and Ruthie, Jodie's brothers and sister, looked like they would never move again.

"I might just be ten," Tom finally spoke through gritted teeth, "but I'm going to find who hurt my brother. When I do, I'm going stick my Buck knife right through his heart." Quick like, he turned his head so nobody could see him cry. Little Ruthie pulled her brown knitted sweater tighter around her.

"I'll help you." James said. Tom was looking far away—didn't even hear him.

One of the ladies from the church came walking across the yard. "Here, you young'uns want some cookies? Baked them myself."

I reached up and took the plate, saying, "Thank you."

"You're welcome, Honey." After she walked away, we passed the plate and sat there eating the oatmeal cookies. I could see Sheriff Harris walk across the porch and shake Uncle Earl's hand. Then the two walked behind the barn.

Soon everybody started dwindling away. Momma was drying the last of the dishes, and Aunt Rosie was lying down. I heard one of the ladies say the medicine Doc Vance had given her would help her sleep.

"Ruthie," Momma said, "why don't you come spend the night with Lily? It'll do you both good, and help your Momma."

"If it's OK with Dad, Aunt Mary," Ruthie replied.

"I'll talk to your Dad. You just get some clothes."

While Ruthie went to get her things, I sneaked to the back door, where I could hear the sheriff and some of the men talking.

"Now, Earl, you calm down. Let's talk about this," the sheriff was saying.

"*Calm down?!* Uncle Earl hissed back. "You tell me to calm down after somebody finds one of *yours* laying half naked, their body trashed by a maniac! See if you can say it *then*! I saw what was done to my little boy; I'm not stupid, Sheriff. If I find him first, I'll chop him up and feed him to the hogs!" By then, Uncle Earl was almost screaming.

"Earl," I heard my dad say gently, "let's go for a walk. Come on, now. Maybe a little drink will calm you down." Sheriff Harris's head was hanging low as Dad led Earl away.

Looking up at the men, the sheriff promised, "Together we will find and punish this lowlife. And when we do, he won't be a man no more. Come on, Fred, we've got a lot of work to do."

My face burned red from what I had heard. *Momma would switch me good if she knew I'd been listening.*

"Lily," my momma called. "Where are you? We're ready to go."

"Right here, Momma. I was getting a drink of water," I said innocently.

"Well come on; run fetch your dad, and tell him to come on."

Me and Ruthie rode in the back of the truck on the way home. The autumn night was still; the halfmoon turned upside down. Dad slowed down once to ask old Jim if he needed a ride.

Jim said, "No, go on Bud. Walk will do me good." Dad gave him a wave and gave the truck some gas. Soon we was pulling up beside the house. Dad helped us down from the truck, then went and opened the door for Momma.

"How 'bout some hot chocolate, girls?" she asked. We both nodded our heads eagerly and smiled. "I'll take that as a yes," she laughed. After the hot cocoa, Momma filled the big washing tub with water and let us bathe while Dad was out putting the cow up. Later, kissing us both on the cheek, she listened to our prayers, then told us to have sweet dreams as she blew the lamp out. We only had electricity in two rooms. Dad said that was all he needed, plus all he could afford. But we were lucky; Dad was one of the few around those parts that had a job, at the saw mill on down the mountain.

In the dark, Ruthie whispered, "Lily, do you think Jodie's an angel?"

"Momma says he is," I answered, "and Momma never lies."

"He was one here to me, Lily. My momma says one day we will all get to see him in heaven."

"I'm sorry you don't have little Jodie no more, Ruthie," I said, and I hugged her tight. Slowly sleep overtook us. The September wind blew a little harder.

Chapter 4

Time crept on. On some days, Momma and I would visit Aunt Rosie, or one of the other mothers would stop in to help with the chores and cooking. Some days she was all right; others she didn't even know you were there. Dad, the sheriff, and a few of the other men had been going around questioning people. Roughing up the younger boys, too, I heard. But no one knew anything. Nobody had seen anyone unusual on Foggy Mountain. Just the same ole people, doing the same ole thing. Old Jim had made his report from the store, and hadn't heard anybody say nothing out of the ordinary. Sheriff Harris and Fred had combed the creek bottom where he was found. The other boys had said they were walking home from playing around in the woods that day. Jodie had been lagging behind, kicking a rock. So they didn't notice that he wasn't behind them 'til they got to where they split up to go to their separate homes. His brothers just thought he had taken a shortcut, trying to beat them home.

"Whoever it was," said Fred, "must have been watching them. Might have been tailing them all day. Jodie would have been an easy target, back there all by himself. Clem, nor any of his boys, hasn't found where anybody had camped or come through the mountains another way. "

Fred looked up at the sky, and then back to the sheriff. "Want to know what I think?"

"Sure, Fred. I need all the help I can get."

"Bill, I think he's right amongst us. A wolf in sheep's clothing, that's what I think. Check out the heavy drinkers around here. Talk to the wives, not the men. See if any of them get a little abusive when they're hitting the bottle."

"Maybe one of them has something to get off their chest... Not a bad idea, Fred. Let's get started. The kids are in school right now, and the men are doing their chores and such. Catching them alone, it'll be easier to talk to them."

Some women were shocked they would even ask such a thing, while others denied their man would even touch a drink. Pretty soon, it was obvious; lips were sealed in a family. If they did know something, they weren't going to tell anybody. That was the mountain way. All the two officers could do was sit back and see if somebody would come to them, and keep their eyes and ears open. Whoever it was had the boys' clothing and shoes. They could just bust every door down and search everybody, but you don't want a mountain full of men with shotguns for enemies. No, keeping on their good side was better. Every tongue got loose once in a while. They'd wait.

School ended for the term in October. Families had to work together to get their tobacco crops in, then handed when it cured. Some grew feed corn; others raised pigs and cattle, so it was slaughtering time, and some were hauled to the sales.

November is an exciting month, Lily thought. *Since my birthday falls the day before Thanksgiving, momma always throws a feast and we celebrate both on Thanksgiving.* When they had gone to town to get her winter shoes, she had spotted a beautiful baby doll. She had told her momma it would be a great birthday present, plus it would teach her how to be a good momma. *Hopefully that last part will give Momma something to think on.* Since Lily's dad worked at the Mill, they didn't raise but just a garden. They bought meat from the farmers. But just the same, her and her momma spent long days digging the potatoes and canning the vegetables. Then they hung the onions and herbs to dry. Next, they wrapped the sweet potatoes in old newspaper to store in the cellar with the others. Jellies sat of rainbow colors on the pantry shelf, ready for a hot biscuit on a cold winter day.

One day Momma had baked a prune cake to take to Ada, little Teddy's momma. She had bought a dime bag of candy to take to the young'uns. Bundling up, we took off walking down the frozen hard dirt road. The shack of a house that Ada lived in looked lonesome and gray. With the trees bare, it was easier to see the big empty fields. Smoke could be seen in the distance, coming from a far-away chimney. In Ada's yard, a few chickens pecked around the barn. Momma knocked gently, and two or three faces pressed up against the window. Ada smiled when she opened the door to see Momma.

She was as frail as a tiny bird, her eyes as empty as the gray sky.

"Come in, Mary, get that girl out of the cold," she said, taking the cake while Momma and I got out of our coats. "Here, let's take this cake in the kitchen. It looks plumb delicious, Mary."

"Stay in here and be good while I visit," Momma said.

"OK, Momma."

Brenda, Ada's oldest girl, was sitting in front of the fireplace holding little Beth, who was just learning to walk. Frankie, who I think was a couple years older than Teddy had been, sat in the corner playing with some blocks of wood. "Come on over and sit by the fire, Lily. Warm yourself up."

Sitting down, I smiled at little Beth. "Want to help me see if we can teach her to walk some?" Brenda asked.

Back and forth we let Beth toddle, from Brenda to me. Sometimes she did good, sometimes she would just plop down and laugh at us. But it was fun just the same. I would have loved to have had a sister, or a brother. Momma always said she reckon God decided I was enough for her and Dad. Still, I wished.

In the kitchen, over a cup of coffee, Ada was telling Momma that they were moving. They were going up North, where her brother lived. John, her husband, was going to get a job in one of those factories. She said, "I just can't stand to sit here another day, Mary, and look out at that field where they found my boy."

"I hate to see you go, Ada, but I guess I can understand, too. We'll miss you something *bad*. Ain't nobody got a singing voice like you, Ada," Momma laughed.

"I know," Ada smiled, and said, "always the big mouth." They both had a laugh, then Ada said, "I want you to do something for me, Mary."

"Sure, anything you ask, Ada."

"Every once in a while, go by Teddy's grave and lay some flowers for me." A tear rolled down her cheek. "And if they ever find that man, write and tell me; I want to know."

"I promise, Ada, I will," Momma gave her friend a tight hug. "Tell Rosie to hang in there. It's hard, I know. Vengeance is the Lord's, and he will repay; tell Rosie that."

Soon Momma was ready to go. We put on our coats and scarves, then hugged everybody bye. Momma reached into her coat pocket and handed the candy to Brenda and Frankie.

"Be a good girl, Lily, and listen to your momma, OK?"

"Yes, Ms. Ada. I will," I replied. The door closed, and we headed back home. Only a little sadder this time.

Chapter 5

Thanksgiving showed up cold and snowy. I was so excited it wouldn't have mattered if it was raining cats. Finally, Momma told me if I didn't quit skipping through the house, the cake was going to fall. Dad came in the back door with a pail of fresh milk and a gust of wind, shaking the snow off his coat.

"Boy, I'm sure glad it's your birthday, Lily. It's the only time a big chocolate cake appears in the pie safe," he laughed.

""You two better get busy, or there won't be anything today," Momma said. "Lily, you help me. Bud, get me some more stove wood before you go get old Jim."

"Yes, Dear." He smiled and winked at me. Every Thanksgiving, the neighbors took turns feeding old Jim dinner. It was the polite thing to do, since he had no family. After getting the stove wood, Dad made sure Momma didn't need anything and went to warm the old truck up. Momma was icing the cake while I jabbed the tater masher up and down in the big pot.

"I'm going, Mary," dad hollered through the house.

"OK; we should be ready before you get back, Bud. Now, young lady, help me set the table, then we'll finish dishing up the food."

After setting the table I looked at Momma with a smile. "Can I get the candle out?" I asked.

"Yes, but don't put it on the cake yet, Lily."

I pulled open the hutch drawer. In the back, wrapped up in a cloth, was the white candle. I laid it excitedly beside the cake.

"Now wash up; I hear your dad coming." Momma smoothed her apron and tidied her hair. "Let's hope old Jim at least took a bath," Momma said.

"He can't help it, Momma. He's old."

"He ain't *that* old," she answered under her breath.

Dad came in, bringing the cold air and old Jim with him. "Hello, Jim. Do you know what today is?" I asked.

"Well, a little birdie told me it was some little girl's birthday," he teased, then grinned at me.

"Yep, I'm nine now!" I gushed.

"You're growing up too fast, Girl." He reached in his pocket and brought out a little brown bag. "Here, just for the birthday girl—but not 'til after dinner, OK?"

"Thank you, Jim. I'll save it, I promise."

"Now, everybody sit down; I might share this dinner Mary scratched up for me," Daddy laughed. The kitchen was toasty. The table held mashed potatoes, corn, beans, sweet potatoes, Momma's fluffy biscuits, and right in the middle, a golden-brown turkey, stuffed. A big bowl of gravy sat beside it. To Momma's relief, old Jim had a new pair of overalls on. Only a musty smell hung around the table.

After we ate. Momma let me place the white candle on top of the cake, then she and dad sang "Happy Birthday" to me.

Blowing out the candle, I looked around to see if a present had appeared.

"If you go look on your bed, I think somebody might have left a good little girl a birthday present," Momma said. I flew to my room. Laying back against my pillow was the baby doll. It simply took my breath away. Her black curls lay softly around her shoulders. The yellow dress had ruffles everywhere. Hugging her tight, I ran back into the kitchen to give Momma and Dad a hug. Then I sat down with my baby, savoring the chocolate cake. Finally, we were all stuffed.

"Better be getting me back home, Bud. Looks like it's going be a big snow," Jim said, wiping his stubby face with his napkin.

"I guess we better, Jim," Dad replied.

"Thanks, Mary, for the meal, and happy birthday, Lily."

"You're welcome," we all chimed in.

"Wait, Jim, I'll fix you a plate for later while the truck warms up," said Momma.

Soon they were out the door. The old truck coughed a little, and the two men went up the road. By now snow was getting heavy on the road, the truck moved slowly.

"So, anybody heard any news on what happened to them young'uns?"

"No, not a word. Jim, it's like the person just vanished after the last time."

"Never know, Bud; he just might have, or could be just waiting. You never know."

"You could be right, Jim, but I'd like to believe he's gone. Then again, I want'em to catch him." "Mmm-hmm," old Jim nodded.

Stopping the truck in the yard, Bud waited 'til he saw the old man go in and shut the door before he started home.

Hope everybody has plenty of firewood, Bud thought. *Probably need to check; take old Jim a load, and maybe sell some. With this weather, the people in town will be buying it up right now.* The old wiper blades barely cleared the window enough for him to see. But soon he spied the soft glow of the lamp through the house window. *Home sweet home.* Bud couldn't wait to get inside and hug the stove.

Chapter 6

November turned into December. Christmas came with a tree Dad found up in the woods above the house. Popcorn and paper ornaments hung on every branch. The church had its Christmas play, and each boy and girl got an orange and apple. Sleds were dragged out. The kids gathered on hills and fields to slide the day away. On the quite cozy days, Momma dropped the quilting frame and showed me how to make the tiny straight stitches, letting me use her old thimble. Dad mostly cut and sold firewood, since the Mill ran slow in the winter; he'd load up the truck, then go into town to sell it. Some of the old people, like old Jim, Dad would just give them a load. Every once in a while, we would visit Aunt Rosie. Us young'uns would go to the barn, play with the kittens, and watch the cows munch on their feed and hay. I got to pick a kitten to take home after its momma weaned it. It was black, with white on each foot. Soon we would get cold and run to the house for hot cocoa, then sit on the floor building things out of the boys' blocks or drawing on the steamed-up window. Nobody was allowed to mention Jodie's name. His coat still hung on the nail by the door. Momma said Aunt Rosie just acted like he was still there: set his plate for supper and washed his clothes, over and over, with the others.

Sheriff Harris had started thinking that maybe it had been a drifter, and now they might get to just forget those awful scenes—but the families would never let him do that. They meant to get justice no matter what the cost, or who it was. He spit the chew he had in his mouth across the frosty ground. Getting into his car he steered it towards Willard's store, thinking *everybody should be gathered around the pot-bellied stove by now.* It was a morning ritual. *Never know, somebody might have heard something.* Walking into the store, the smell of sawdust, leather, and spices welcomed him. Sure enough, there they sat. The old cane-bottom chairs were drawn up in a circle around the stove, the elders sitting, the farmers leaning. The sheriff nodded to Willard as he walked by the counter.

"'Whatcha say, Bill?" bellowed Hubert Jenkins, adjusting his hands in his front pockets. Every head was adorned with a Co-op or a Big Berley hat, or one from Willard's feed and seed.

"Take a rest, Sheriff," old Jim grinned.

"Might do that," the sheriff answered, pulling an apple crate over to the stove. "What're you all jawing about this morning?" he asked.

"Ah, old Jim was just bragging how he was going be turning seventy soon, and probably could still outwork us young goats," Hubert laughed, giving old Jim's shoulder a shake.

"Land sakes, he can barely walk," Sheriff Harris said, joining in on the joke. Old Jim just looked at him and winked with a grin.

Talk was the usual, for a while: getting 'bout plowing time; bet it'll be a hot summer; wonder what seed prices will be this year. Just the usual. Walking up to the counter, Sheriff Harris laid his money down for the grape soda.

"I ain't heard nothing either, Sheriff," Willard spoke, giving the sheriff an understanding look.

"Well, if you do, you know where to find me, Willard. Take care."

"You too, Sheriff."

The hands of time kept on turning on the big clock of life. Soon February gave way to March, and it came in like a lion. Wind and rain one day, snow and sleet the next. You never know about March. The plowed fields where hard frozen clumps of dirt now. Then the sun would come out, and the ground was a soft mud.

Lily was glad to be back in school after being cooped up all winter. Being nine years old, she got to move farther back in the one-room school house, with the older kids. Momma had made her a new spring dress and she hated having to cover it with a coat when she walked to school. The tan cloth held a print of all kinds of tiny spring flowers all over it. It was beautiful, and soft touching her skin. During lunch she sat with Tom, James, and Ruthie on a big rock while the sun warmed them like a blanket.

After school they all walked home together, stopping at Lily's house first; then on up the road the trio went, to Aunt Rosie's house. Tom still didn't talk much. Time don't heal all wounds.

Chapter 7

He felt the cool breeze sweep into the room through the open window. Sitting in the middle of the bed, he ran his hands gently over the denim cloth, excitement running through his body like electricity. His heart pounded as he tied and untied the little boot on his lap. His body was a storm now. Picking up the small pants, he held them close to his face, inhaling the fragrance in slow breaths. Shutting his eyes, he waited 'til his thoughts left his body weak. Then, slow and gently, he folded the clothing and placed it, with the shoes on top, back into the box. Lifting the loose board in the floor, he set the box on the cold ground, letting the board fall back in place to hide it. Once again, he reached for the jar and drank 'til a different heat overtook him. His dreams were sweet, his body numb.

Fred stood on the front porch with his wife Sadie.

"Not as cold out tonight, Hon."

"No, spring is just around the corner," she agreed, then smiled. "You're going to have to hire one of Clem's boys to come plow the garden, since you're still hobbling on that foot."

"Yeah, I guess so. Doc says it's 'bout healed. I know Bill's tired of doing everything hisself." He laughed. "You know what, Sadie? I still think he's looking the wrong way on finding the person that murdered those boys."

"What do you mean, Fred?"

"Well, he still thinks it was a drifter. I think he's right here, amongst us. Watching and listening, probably laughing that he got away with it."

"Surely not, Fred. Why, I don't know a person around here that would do such things to a young'un."

"That's what they *want* you to think. That way, nobody would suspect a thing. I've been watching some; watching them *real* close. Now, let's get in the house before we get a spring chill." He held the screen door open for her, giving one last look at the black sky. Not long after laying down, he heard the pitter-patter of rain on the roof. He went over every face of every man on the mountain in his mind, trying to picture one of them doing what had been done to those boys. But nothing stuck out. *I'm missing something, have to be. I won't stop* he thought, and turned over, waiting for sleep.

March ended like a lamb. The sun was warmer. The ground had dried enough to get a horse and disk plow through. Work always seemed to lift the tension of anything. At night, you were too tired to lay in bed and think. Mary, like every other woman, was planting her garden. She hoed it 'til the dirt was like shifted flour. Lily dropped seed potatoes in, while her momma covered them. She wasn't allowed to put her shoes away just yet; Momma said the ground still held a chill. But oh, how she would have loved to bury her feet in the soft dirt. There were two more months of school, and then freedom. After chores she could play with her cat, swing on the old tire Dad had hung in the tree out back...might even build a tree house.

"Pay attention, Lily," her momma reminded her. "Your mind's wandering again."

"Yes, Momma," Lily responded, and she dropped another seed potato. Next would be the corn, beans, and onions. Dad was back working at the sawmill, or else he would be here helping.

Seemed like every little creature had babies now. The hens had little doodles all over the barnyard. Baby birds chirped hungrily for their mommas to hurry back with food. Hopefully Brownie, their old milk cow, would soon give birth to a baby herself.

"That's all for now, Lily," Momma sighed. "You go rinse the dirt off your shoes, and then you can go play."

Lily took off to the water bucket out back to rinse her shoes. Then she went to find Mittens, her cat, to go swing with her for a while. *I sure do hate not being able to just take off somewhere to play anymore,* she thought. Momma and Dad still wouldn't allow her to go alone anywhere. *Maybe before long they won't be so worried.* Kicking off with her feet, she closed her eyes and let the tire swing her through the wind and warm sunshine. Mittens hung on for dear life.

Chapter 8

School's out, school's out, teacher let the monkeys out," could be heard all over the schoolyard that day after school. Lily and Ruthie quickly sat down, laughing, at the edge of the yard, pulling the heavy brogan shoes off and stuffing their socks inside, before running after Tom and James down the road towards home.

"Hey Ruthie, why don't you ask your momma if you can spend the night pretty soon?" Lily asked.

"She probably would let me, we done got all the planting done. Just ask Aunt Mary to make sure I can."

"I will, as soon as I get home."

"Who's that sitting up there on that stump?" James asked, squinting at the sun.

"Nobody important." Tom muttered, "just old Jim."

"Hey there, young'uns! School out already?" Jim asked.

"Hey there, Jim. Yep, we're out for the summer," James answered

"Well, I'll be." Jim grinned, then said, "Well, come here; I might have something for a bright bunch like you." Walking over to the stump, they waited while Jim slowly rose. Reaching in his pocket he pulled out a sucker for each one.

"Thanks, Jim!" they all chimed.

"You're welcome. Now get on home, before your mommas get worried about you."

"Yes, Sir." Walking slower now, they savored the sweet cherry flavor.

"I wish all the old people were as nice as Jim," James sputtered between licks.

"Why, so your teeth could rot out?" Tom laughed. Lily smiled just to hear Tom laugh. Maybe it would be a great summer, like old times, after all.

"See you all later," Lily told her cousins when they got to her yard. "Don't forget to ask your momma, Ruthie."

"I won't, and don't forget to ask yours, Lily."

"I won't," Lily sang, as she went skipping through the yard. "I'm home, Momma!"

"Get out of your good dress before you do anything, Young Lady."

"Yes, Momma," she smiled as she gave her momma a hug. *Yum*, she thought as she changed dresses. *Something smells good!* As she entered the kitchen, Momma was pouring a clear syrup over a cake.

"What kind is it?" Lily asked.

"Gingerbread, your daddy's favorite."

"Can I lick the pan?"

"Sure; be careful, though. The pan's still a little hot."

Lily took her finger and tested the pan before swiping up the sweet syrup. "Momma, do you think Ruthie could spend the night pretty soon, since school's out?"

"Don't see why not, as long as her momma says it's OK."

"Thanks, Momma."

"Now, go get washed up for supper. Your dad will be here soon."

The next Friday , Aunt Rosie let Ruthie come spend the night with Lily. Momma popped them popcorn. They played on the bed with Lily's doll; Lily never took her outside. Then the girls giggled half the night, 'til Momma had to hush them. The next morning, they gathered the eggs and helped set the table for breakfast. They played all day. Later that evening, Momma said it was time for Ruthie to get ready to go home.

"Can I walk her home, Momma?"

"I don't know, Lily; you would have to walk back by yourself."

"I'll be careful, and I'll even run if you want me to."

Momma thought for a minute. OK, Lily, but you go straight there and back, you hear?"

"I will, I promise," Lily swore.

"Bye, Aunt Mary, thanks for letting me stay," said Ruthie.

"You're welcome, Sweetheart. Now give me a kiss before you go."

Letting the screen door slam behind them, they set off for Ruthie's house. Walking up the road, they picked Aunt Rosie some honeysuckle blooms to go on her table. At Ruthie's porch, Lily said bye and thanked Aunt Rosie for letting her stay.

"Lily, I don't like you walking home alone. Tom and James are out looking for rabbits, or I'd make Tom walk you," Rosie said.

"I'll be OK, Aunt Rosie. I'm going hurry straight back." Aunt Rosie watched her 'til she was out of sight.

Walking along, Lily carried a stick and ran it through the tall grass that grew on the side of the road as she went. Looking over to her right, she could see Mr. Tate's cattle grazing way out in the pasture. She hadn't taken maybe five more steps when she heard a rustling sound to her left, off the bank.

Slowing she listened; something was moaning, but then something was breathing hard, too. Looking around, Lily thought if she was quiet enough, she might could peek at what it was.

Taking slow, tiny steps, she went through the grass and down the bank a little. It was so grown up it was hard to see. Squatting down, she looked as hard as she could through the brush. She could still hear the breathing, but the moaning had stopped. Then, down where the wet spring ran, she saw a figure leaned over. *Oh! It's somebody sick*, Lily thought. She stepped on around the brush to see if they needed her to get help. Looking at the ground beside the figure, she saw an old gray hat. *Oh lord, its old Jim!* As she slipped and half-fell getting down the bank, she hollered, "Hold on, Jim! I'm coming! You OK?" In a million years, Lily would never forget the face that turned to her. Almost to him, she stopped dead in her tracks. The eyes were wild and glassy. His face was an alarming reddish-purple color, and sweat was running in little streams down his neck. On his knees, he leaned back and spit dripped off his chin. One hand was holding something down, the other was pointing at her. Lily's legs went weak as water. Jumping up, he grabbed her around the waist. As he did, her eyes fell on the ground in front of Jim. In a flash, her eyes saw the most horrible thing ever to be seen. The little boy lay pressed face down in mud from the spring. She got one scream out before a rough hand covered her mouth. Vomit rose up in her throat at the smell.

"You picked a bad day to go for a walk, Little Girl. Quit your squirming; won't do you no good." Lily's mind went black with fear. At first, she thought she had passed out—but then she felt her body hit the ground hard. She could hear, but didn't want to look. Her face was wet with tears and the taste of blood was in her mouth.

"I got you! You dirty dog!" Lily heard, and in an instant, she knew the voice. Raising up on her elbow, she saw Tom on top of old Jim. He had bashed the old man's head with a rock 'cause, it was still in his hand. Jim lay there trying to get a hold of himself, but it was too late. In Tom's other hand, Lily saw the shiny blade of his Buck knife coming down. He buried it plumb up to the handle in Jim's chest. Lily was still crying and shaking When Tom turned to look at her, never getting off Jim. Tears ran down his face, his teeth were gritted together, and his hand still gripped the knife handle.

"Get out of here, Lily!" he cried. "Don't look, just hurry and go get help!" On my hands and knees, I crawled back up the bank. I didn't even feel the rocks and brush tearing at my flesh. When I reached the road, I ran.

Chapter 9

Reaching our porch, I fell trying to get up the steps. I gasped for breath to scream for Momma, but she had heard me moan when I hit the steps.

"Oh, my god! Lily!" she cried. Quickly she picked me up.

"What happened? Tell me what happened!"

Through my sobs, I finally got out, "Help Tom, Momma; help Tom."

"Oh, my lord," she repeated over and over as she started out to the road, still holding me. I lay drained against my momma's body. Her arms held me tightly to her chest, shaking. Then I heard my dad's truck. When he saw us in the road he jumped out, not even putting the truck in park.

"What's wrong, Mary?" His voice broke, he was so worried.

"She keeps saying help Tom," Momma cried.

"Where's he at, Honey?" Dad asked, moving my hair away from my face. "Hurry and tell Daddy so I can help him," he said, his eyes beginning to water.

"Up the road, Daddy," I cried. "Off the bank were the wet spring is." He ran back to his truck. It had rolled back to the side of the road, where the fence post had stopped it.

"Get her in the house, Mary," he shouted as he floored the truck up the road.

Momma ran with me still in her arms back into the house, her breathing heavy with panic. Locking the door behind us, she took me in the kitchen and sat me on the table. Taking my face in her hands first, she checked every spot on me, quick as a flash.

"Are you hurt anywhere, Lily?" her hands trembled as she raised my dress to check my legs.

"Just a little, Momma," I cried. "Tom saved me, Momma. He stopped him." Her eyes were wide open with fear.

"Sit still," she ordered, "I'm going to get a wet cloth." She grabbed a dish rag and dipped it into the water reservoir, warm from the cook stove's heat. After wiping my face and arms she went to the cabinet, bringing back a bottle of brown liquid and a spoon.

"Here, take this." I opened my mouth, swallowing the spoonful of liquid. For a second, I couldn't get my breath—but soon I felt warm all over, and the shaking slacked off some. "Now," she said taking me by the shoulders and looking me in the eye, "tell me what happened, Lily." I hadn't opened my mouth yet when we heard the sheriff's car go by, with the siren screaming.

Bud had parked the truck off the road as much as he could. Jumping out, he frantically started looking off the road through the trees, yelling for Tom as he walked. After going quite a few feet, he finally heard Tom. "Here, Uncle Bud! I'm down here!"

Bud tore down the bank. Tom still sat on the man's chest, his hand still wrapped around the knife handle. Bud looked around wildly, trying to take in the scene. His first thought was the young boy still holding the knife.

"It's OK now, Tom. I'm here, you can let go." Tom, at the tender age of eleven, looked up at his uncle.

"I got him, Uncle Bud! He was going hurt Lily too, but I got him."

"Yes, you did, Son. Now let go of the knife, and let me help you up."

"If he moves, Uncle Bud, you stab him again! That's the devil there."

"I will; I promise, Tom. Here, give me your hand." Reaching out, Bud took the boy's hand and lifted him off the man. Tom wrapped his arms around Bud's waist, and Bud held him tight. Looking down at the man, past the bloody face, Bud saw that it was old Jim. Out from his body lay another, much smaller. Black and blue, his face was almost completely hidden in the marshy mud from the spring water.

"We need to get the sheriff, Tom."

"James went, Uncle Bud," he answered, raising his tear-streaked face. "We was hunting rabbits when we heard Lily scream. We thought a snake had got her, so we ran down here."

"Come on," Bud said, "let's get to the road so we can see them coming." Bud already heard the sheriff's car. "Don't look back, Tom; it's over. Climb on my back." Through the brush and up the bank Bud went, with Tom on his back.

When he got to the truck, he saw half a dozen men coming in a rush. The sheriff parked in a cloud of dust. Bud sat Tom on the tailgate, placing a hand on either side of him. The sheriff jumped out of the car and hurried up to the truck.

"What happened, Bud?" Sheriff Harris asked. He looked around and saw all the other men approaching. Bud wiped the sweat from his face with his shirttail.

"It's all down there, Sheriff. That's all I can say."

Sheriff Harris patted Bud on the back and turned to the men. "Come on, let's see what's happened. Everybody stay calm, don't get hot headed on me now. Don't worry, Tom; I had Fred walk James back home."

"Thank you, Sheriff," Tom mumbled. Bud watched the men go over the bank.

He heard her before he even saw her.

Rosie came running down the road, screaming for Tom. "Here, Rosie; he's right here. Don't worry, he's OK," Bud soothed Rosie as she hugged her boy tight. Poor Rosie looked as if she was reliving Jodie's death.

"Where's Lily, Bud?" Tears poured down her pale face.

"Lily's OK, Rosie. She's with her momma. Tom here saved Lily; he was a brave boy."

"Oh, lord! Tom, you sure you're OK?"

"Yes, Momma. Where's Dad?" he asked, wiping his nose and eyes on her apron.

"He went around the back way; said he could get there quicker."

"Rosie, why don't you take Tom home? I'm sure the sheriff will be by later to talk to him and get the whole story. I'll go get Mary and Lily, and bring them to your house."

"OK, Bud," Rosie agreed.

"You all right to walk back, Rosie?"

"Yeah I'll be fine; I'll be waiting for Mary." Rosie kept her arm around Tom as they walked around the truck, past the newly beaten-down trail that lead off the road, on towards home. Turning the truck around, Bud headed home to get Mary and to make sure his baby was OK. Then they would all go to Rosie's.

Chapter 10

The sheriff and other men had a hard time figuring it all out, at first. Earl and Fred had come down from the other side.

"Does anybody know what happened here?" the sheriff asked. *My lord*, he thought. *Looks like somebody went mad!*

"I know a little, Sheriff," Earl spoke up. "James said him and Tom heard Lily scream, thought a snake or something had got her. When they ran down here, old Jim had hold of her. Had her mouth covered, and she was crying. Then Tom seen the little boy, and knew what he had done. He grabbed a rock and jumped on him from behind, bashing his head. Old Jim dropped Lily when he fell down. I guess after that, Tom made good on his promise; he took his knife and stabbed him through the heart, and sent James to get you. What happened before that I guess only Lily knows."

Fred looked at old Jim lying there, soaked in blood. *He was right in amongst us*, he thought. *I was right.*

"Does anybody know the boy?" the sheriff asked.

Hubert squatted down and gently rolled the boy over. Taking his handkerchief out of his back pocket, he wiped the mud away from the boy's face. "It's Jake, Hattie's boy. Remember, his daddy died last year, when that log fell on him."

"What do you want us to do now, Sheriff?" one of the men asked.

"First, some of you men get that boy up out of here," the sheriff said, angry now. Gently, Hubert and Clem laid little Jake onto a shirt someone had tossed them. As they walked by with the boy, Sheriff Harris noticed the clutched fist. "Hold on," he said, pulling the small fingers loose. There in his palm lay several pieces of candy corn. The orange candy had melted and smeared between the small fingers. A few pieces fell, landing at the toe of the sheriff's boot. "Go ahead," he seethed. And up the bank they went.

The silence was heavy. Fred, Earl, and JD stood waiting on the sheriff to speak. Earl was standing nearby, looking down hard at the man that had took his boy. Fred bent down, and reaching into Jim's pocket he pulled out a worn brown paper bag. Opening it up, he saw the same kind of candy that little Jake had been holding in his hand.

Sheriff Harris finally spoke. "Earl..."

"Yeah, Bill?" he answered.

"Remember what you said you would do to the man, if you found him?"

"Yes, Sir. I do," Earl said, looking up at the sheriff.

"Go feed your hogs, then. I'm sure somebody will help you. Come on Fred, they don't need us here." The sheriff walked away, back up to the road.

"We'll go on up and talk to Tom, make sure they're OK. Then we'll head on over to Hattie's."

"Sure," Fred agreed.

They didn't speak on the short drive up the road. When they got to Rosie's, Lily explained what had happened to the sheriff. Then Tom told his part.

"Tom," the sheriff said firmly to the boy, "don't ever feel bad about what you did. Just like David when he slew the giant, you did a brave thing."

"What about the boy?" Tom asked.

"There's nothing we can do to help him now, Son, but thanks to you there won't be another one." Shaking the young boy's hand, Sheriff Harris and Fred said their goodbyes and headed to their last sad visit, Hattie's.

"Let's get this over with, Fred. Then I'm finding another job."

"Don't blame you none on that, Bill. Nope, not at all," Said Fred.

Hattie was a mess when they left her. She found some comfort in knowing the man who took her little boy was dead. Her sister had come to wait for the body with her.

Tomorrow the men on Foggy Mountain will gather again, to dig another grave. Who would have thought... Fred always believed it was somebody amongst us; guess he was right.

But old Jim! The man always looked like he couldn't hurt a cat, let alone a young'un. Just goes to show you how good you know people, he thought. Going down the road, he looked over at Fred.

"You ready to go see what we find, Fred?"

"I don't know if I want to know," Fred answered. "No way getting out of it, I reckon."

"Nope." The sheriff let out a long breath.

Pulling into the half-barren, half-grass yard, the sheriff stopped the car in a puff of dust. Both men got out and walked to the front of the car. Leaning back against the hood, they observed the rickety old house.

"You know, I don't think I've ever been in there, in all these years I've known him," Fred finally said.

"Well...it's been a long time for me, Fred. The times I did come by to check on him, he most always came out."

"I always thought he was a little ashamed of the place, so I didn't push him." Fred sighed. "Let's go, Bill; let's get it over with. Makes me sick just to look at the house."

The sheriff opened the weathered wooden door. Fred was close behind. The small kitchen had a dim light coming through the grease and smoke that had collected over the years on the old window.

"Light that oil lamp, Fred. I didn't think to bring a light."

Picking up a box of matches, Fred lifted the globe and put the flame to the wick. Both men stood in the middle of the room and looked around. The fire in the cook stove was just embers now. Pans with leftover food sat in a scattered heap. Some even had dust on the handles. A bowl, plates, and used drinking cups sat on the table, floor, and window sill. One door to the right led to the only other room in the house. Picking up the oil lamp Sheriff Harris slowly opened it, holding the lamp high.

The first thing that hit them was the smell. Fred quickly took his handkerchief from his back pocket and tied it around his mouth and nose. Moving the lamp around the room, the sheriff could see a bed and one dresser. An old crate sat beside the bed, with a mason jar on it.

"Dear lord. It smells like a pack of dogs have been shut up in here," the sheriff gasped. "I would bet my life that sheet and quilt ain't never been washed."

Fred lit the other lamp on the dresser. A pile of moldy clothes filled one comer. The window had a piece of burlap nailed across it. Other than that, the room was empty. They opened the drawers of the dresser, finding nothing but some old papers and junk. Getting on his knees, the sheriff bent down to look under the bed. Nothing but cob webs and dust were there. He threw back the quilt to find nothing but a soiled mattress and sheet. Fred walked around the bed, looking at the walls and floor. At the head of the bed, in the corner, he saw a board that was wider than the rest.

"Hey, Bill, come here. I think I found something." Walking around to where Fred was, the sheriff looked down. "See that board?" Fred asked, pointing. "It's wider." Once again, the sheriff got down on the floor. Taking his knife out, he put the blade between the boards and flipped the wide one up. Sure enough, something was in there. Sliding the lamp closer to the opening, he could see an old pasteboard box. The edges were frayed and worn. Carefully, with both hands, he lifted it out.

Fred knelt on the other side of the box. Slowly the sheriff lifted the lid off. Sitting neatly on top were a pair of little patched boots, strings neatly tied in a bow. "Sweet *lord*," Fred breathed. The sheriff's hands were shaking as he put them down on his thighs. Folded beneath the boots was a pair of handmade overalls, a pair of socks, and a little torn flannel shirt.

"We just opened the devil's box, Fred. He took something from each boy, like a *trophy*," Sheriff Harris spat.

Fred just stared hard at the small pile. "What now?" he asked. Getting up, the sheriff stood with the lamp in his hand. Fred joined him.

"Come on, Fred," the sheriff said, walking back to the bedroom door. After Fred was out of the room, Sheriff Harris raised the lamp one more time.

Next thing Fred heard was it crashing against the wall at the head of the bed. The flames licked at the oil as it ran down the wall; soon the bed and walls were covered with raging flames. Shutting the door, he reached for Fred's lamp.

"Go on out, Fred," he said. Fred stepped out into the yard, and soon he heard the other lamp crash against a wall. Both men walked to the car. Leaning back against the hood this time, they watched as the house was slowly engulfed in flames.

"It can all burn in hell now," Sheriff Harris declared. "Let's go, Fred." Backing out, they watched as the black smoke rolled up to the sky. When the bedroom window exploded, the sheriff smiled. He could almost hear the boys laughing, and see them watching it burn.

This story is dedicated to my grandson, Jackson.

"Hush Little Baby"

Hush little baby, don't you cry...
One of these days
all pain will subside...
You'll be OK, this I know...
'Cause in the Bible he tells us so...
So hush little baby and don't you cry;
He will wipe all the tears from your eyes.

—E.B.

About the Author

Elizabeth Hardin Buttke holds a diploma in Medical Records and was also a substitute teacher. She has written stories and poems for her family since a young girl. *Deep in the Holler* is her first published book of some of the wonderful stories of her childhood. You may contact her through Facebook, or email at: ebuttke@yahoo.com.